# Goodnight Ellie, Goodnight Marguerite

## A Baby Book for Best Cousins

Written by Kevin Jolivette

To my daughter, Marguerite,
and her cousin, Ellie.

Two baby cousins,
Born minutes but many miles apart.

Although the distance was far,
Their families wanted them close at heart.

With one in the mountains,
And the other in the plains,

The parents did their best,
Using technological gains.

So every night,
Once bundled and clean,

The baby cousins would stare at each other,
But only through a computer screen.

The parents would talk about firsts,
And what each liked to eat.

But the calls always ended with,
"Goodnight Ellie, Goodnight Marguerite."

Then when schedules allowed,
And the families could meet,

The parents laid them side-by-side whispering,
"Goodnight Ellie, Goodnight Marguerite."

And when they visited Nana,
Who always spoiled them with a treat,

They'd share the same room and say,
"Goodnight Ellie, Goodnight Marguerite."

And even at summer camp,
After meeting friends and trying new feats,

The teenagers would bunk together and say,
"Goodnight Ellie, Goodnight Marguerite."

And when one was starring in high school plays,
While the other a great athlete,

They'd call each other every night and say,
"Goodnight Ellie, Goodnight Marguerite."

And when they roomed together in college,
With one overly messy and the other way too neat,

They still ended every night with,
"Goodnight Ellie, Goodnight Marguerite."

And when they moved to start their careers,
One in the courtroom and the other on Wall Street,

They called to wish good luck and say,
"Goodnight Ellie, Goodnight Marguerite."

And when they started their own families,
Being miles apart didn't make it at all bittersweet,

Because they called each other nightly to say...

**"Goodnight Ellie,
Goodnight Marguerite."**

Made in the USA
Middletown, DE
29 November 2020